MY LiFe as a Mixed-Up Millennium Bug

BOOKS BY BILL MYERS

Children's Series
The Incredible Worlds of Wally McDoogle:
—*My Life As a Smashed Burrito with Extra Hot Sauce*
—*My Life As Alien Monster Bait*
—*My Life As a Broken Bungee Cord*
—*My Life As Crocodile Junk Food*
—*My Life As Dinosaur Dental Floss*
—*My Life As a Torpedo Test Target*
—*My Life As a Human Hockey Puck*
—*My Life As an Afterthought Astronaut*
—*My Life As Reindeer Road Kill*
—*My Life As a Toasted Time Traveler*
—*My Life As Polluted Pond Scum*
—*My Life As a Bigfoot Breath Mint*
—*My Life As a Blundering Ballerina*
—*My Life As a Screaming Skydiver*
—*My Life As a Human Hairball*
—*My Life As a Walrus Whoopee Cushion*
—*My Life As a Mixed-Up Millennium Bug*

McGee and Me! (12 books)

Bloodhounds, Inc. (5 books)

Teen Series
Forbidden Doors (10 books)

Teen Nonfiction
Hot Topics, Tough Questions
Faith Encounters

Picture Book
Baseball for Breakfast

Adult Fiction
Blood of Heaven
Threshold
Fire of Heaven

Adult Nonfiction
Christ B.C.
The Dark Side of the
Supernatural

the incredible worlds of **Wally McDoogle**

MY LiFe

as a

Mixed-Up

Millennium
Bug

BILL MYERS

Tommy
NELSON™

Thomas Nelson, Inc.

Nashville

MY LIFE AS A MIXED-UP MILLENNIUM BUG

Published in Nashville, Tennessee, by Tommy Nelson™, a division of Thomas Nelson, Inc.

Unless otherwise indicated, Scripture quotations are from the *International Children's Bible, New Century Version,* copyright © 1983, 1986, 1988.

Library of Congress Cataloging-in-Publication Data

Myers, Bill, 1953–
   My life as a mixed-up millennium bug / Bill Myers.
      p. cm. — (The incredible worlds of Wally McDoogle ; #17)
   Summary: When inept Wally McDoogle discovers that whatever he types on his computer turns into reality, what starts as just a little cheating soon escalates into a war.
   ISBN 0-8499-4026-5
[1. Computers Fiction. 2. Cheating Fiction. 3. Humorous stories.] I. Title. II. Series: Myers, Bill, 1953– Incredible worlds of Wally McDoogle ; #17.
PZ7.M98234Mm   1999
[Fic]—dc21   99-35244
                                               CIP

Printed in the United States of America
00 01 02 03 QPV 9 8 7 6 5 4

To Nancy Rue—
Another friend committed to reaching youth

"The LORD detests lying lips, but he delights in men who are truthful."

—Proverbs 12:22 (NIV)

Contents

Chapter 1

Just for Starters . . .

So what's so wrong with a little cheating? You know, scribbling an answer or two on your wrist before the test, or embroidering them on the back of the shirt of the person sitting in front of you. Then, of course, there's the ol' standby of hiring a sky writer to scrawl the answers up there in the sky so as you gaze out the window you just happen to come up with all the right answers.

So what's the matter with that?

Unfortunately, I found out the answer the hard way: **PLENTY!**

Oh, sorry, didn't mean to shout. I guess I just don't want you to have to go through what I did. Not that you could; after all, there's only one Wally The-Walking-Disaster McDoogle. But still . . .

It all started with P.E., which, as everyone knows, stands for *Physical Embarrassment*. Once again Coach Kilroy (whose name could just as easily be Coach Kill-Wally) was on my case. All year he'd been threatening to flunk me. That's why Mom and Dad suggested I take the special course he was offering over the winter break for extra credit. It sounded great, except for the part where I actually had to go to class.

"Come on, McDoogle! Stop being a wimp and climb that rope! You're holding up the line! Climb the rope!"

It was all part of an elaborate obstacle course Coach had set up outside on the soccer field. "To get you ready for the big computer crash," he shouted. "When that Y2K bug hits and there's rioting in the streets, you'll thank your lucky stars that I made you tough enough to survive!"

That was Coach's new mission in life . . . to help us survive some sort of big, worldwide computer crash. I appreciated the thought, but right now I just wanted to survive the last eighteen minutes of class.

I'd been hanging on to that rope, trying to climb it, for just a little past forever. But with no success. (Unless you call my arms stretching a good foot and a half longer than they're supposed to "success.") It's not that I'm a wimp—shoot, sometimes I work out for hours on end . . . if you call pushing all those buttons on the TV remote "working out"!

"Forget it, McDoogle!" Coach finally shouted. "Move on to the next station! Move it! Move it! Move it!"

Gratefully, I "moved it" and ran to the next station in the obstacle course . . . dragging my newly stretched arms on the ground behind me.

Unfortunately, this station was no better. We were to run through eight tires and up to a giant wall with a fishing net and then climb it. Well, everyone else was running through the eight tires up to the giant wall with the fishing net and climbing it. I, on the other hand, was stepping into one tire and

"Whoa!"
K-Flop

falling on my face. Then stepping into the next one and

"Whoa!"
K-Flop

falling on my face.

Of course, Coach was shouting his usual encouragement, "McDoogle, you moron!" but I wasn't worried. I knew I'd make it to the wall before nightfall.

"Whoa!"
K-Flop
"Whoa!"
K-Flop

I just wasn't sure which night.

Anyway, after running through the eight tires with my mandatory eight falls, I finally made it to the wall. It was kind of weak and wobbly, since Coach had just built it the day before, but that wasn't my concern. All I had to do was put my foot in the netting and pull myself up. There, that wasn't so hard. Just put my other foot in the netting and . . . uh-oh. I don't know how I did it, but in 1.3 seconds I managed to get myself slightly stuck. In another 2.6 seconds I got myself majorly stuck.

"McDoogle!" Coach was definitely not happy.

I tried harder, squirming and wiggling, but the more I wiggled the more tangled I got. Finally, I'd turned the nice fish netting into some sort of knotted up crochet.

"McDOOGLE!!"

Fortunately, Wall Street, my best friend, even if she is a girl, was also taking the course, and she raced to my side to help. Over the years she's had lots of experience in getting me out of problems. "Come on, Wally," she said. "We don't want Coach to flunk you. Just put your foot there . . . no, there . . . NO, Wally, *there* . . ."

Unfortunately, her version of *there* was slightly different from mine . . . which meant we soon turned that nice piece of crochet I had made into an even nicer knitted sweater.

"McDOOGLE!!"

So there I was, dangling upside down from the fishing net doing my best imitation of a human piñata, when my other best friend, Opera, who was also taking the course, came on the scene. Not only does Opera love classical music (which explains the Walkman headphones surgically attached to his ears), but he also loves junk food (which explains why he weighs just slightly less than a Mack truck).

"Here, Wally," he shouted. "Grab my hands and I'll pull you down."

It wasn't a bad idea—and thanks to my newly stretched arms I was able to reach down to him. He grabbed my hands and began to pull.

No problem . . . except for Opera's weight . . . and the weak, wobbly wall . . . and all that pulling.

creak . . . groan

"What's that?" I yelled.
"Don't know!" he shouted and pulled harder.

Creak . . . Groan

"Uh, Opera?"
More pulling.

CREAK . . . GROAN

"Oh, Opera?"
Until, finally . . .

C R E A K . . .
G R O A N . . .

the entire wall started to fall.
"Look out!" Wall Street cried. "It's coming down!"
She was right. The wall and I were falling straight toward the ground. For one terrifying second I was afraid I'd be smashed flatter than a tortilla hit by a semi carrying a load of sumo wrestlers . . . until I saw the tires.

The good news was the wall and I weren't going to hit the ground at all. We were going to land right on the tires . . . right on those nice rubbery, bouncy tires. And I was right, they were nice, rubbery, and

Boing!

bouncy. So bouncy that as soon as I hit them I
flew back up and out of the net. Not, of course,
without accidentally getting my leg stuck in one
of the tires and sort of pulling it up with me.
Once again I came back down, this time landing
on my own private tire, and once again

Boing!

I flew back up.
   So there I was,

bounce . . . bounce . . . bouncing . . .

across the soccer field like a giant basketball,
when I realized two very important facts:

1. I was about to run out of the nice, soft soccer field, and
2. My next stop would be the not-so-nice (and
definitely not-so-soft) teachers' parking lot.

I knew I had to protect myself from all that
asphalt and gravel, so I decided to curl up inside
my tire and ride it out until we finally stopped
bouncing.
   The good news was the bouncing eventually

stopped. The bad news was we quit bouncing and
started to

> *ROLL . . . ROLL...ROLL...*
> *ROLLROLLROLLROLL . . .*

faster and faster and faster some more. Soon,
everything was a spinning blur—the trees, the
cars, the school wall.

THE SCHOOL WALL!

Ah, yes, the school

> *K-RASH!*

wall.

  Fortunately, that was about all I remembered
from Coach's little Y2K training. It's hard to
remember anything when you've been totally
knocked out. However, before I slipped into uncon-
scious-ville, I did remember thinking something
else . . . I remembered thinking I might not exactly
be getting an A in P.E.

  Unfortunately, I couldn't have been more
wrong . . .

* * * * *

Six hours later I lay in bed, milking my injuries for all they were worth. You know the routine . . . "Oh, Mom, could you get this? Oh, Mom, could you get that?" And if she hesitates, just put a bit more whine in your voice and bingo: instant parent slave.

Good ol' Mom . . . works every time.

Unfortunately, it's not quite the same with Dad. It seems every time I complain to him about a broken body part, he jokingly offers to break something else to help take my mind off the pain.

Good ol' Dad.

Anyway, since dinner was about to be served (in bed, of course), I decided to kill a little time by writing one of my superhero stories. Someday I hope to be a writer . . . if I can live through the seventh grade . . . and Coach Kilroy's class.

I got up, strolled over to my desk, fed my fish, checked out my science project of living cockroaches in a terrarium (hey, everybody needs a hobby), and whipped out Ol' Betsy, my laptop computer. Finally, I turned her on and got to work:

It has been another super swell day for the stunningly stupendous and superb superhero...Chocolate Chum. Already he has talked a well-known restaurant chain

into replacing all its maple syrup
with chocolate syrup (ever try chocolate-
covered waffles?...Don't!); convinced a
local broccoli farm to start selling
chocolate-covered broccoli (Double
Don't!); and broken up a half-dozen
Chocoholic Anonymous meetings by standing up and shouting, "Hi, my name's
Choco Chum, I'm a Chocoholic...AND I'M
PROUD OF IT!"

Now, with the satisfaction that he has
again made the world a sweeter, sweller,
and just a little bit chubbier place to
live, our hero pops out his microwave
meal of spaghetti and fudge balls
(smothered in extra chocolate sauce) and
waddles over to turn on the TV.

But instead of his favorite game show,
Wheel of Chocolate, there's a bunch of
crazed overweight guys yelling and jabbing their fingers at each other. "Oh,
brother," our hero groans, "it's another
political debate"...until he realizes
these guys aren't politicians, but professional wrestlers.

He switches channels.

But it's the same thing. Instead of

Touched by a Chocolate Bar, it's another wrestling match.

He switches again. Now, instead of that famous purple fudgesicle singing, "I love you, you love me," there's even more wrestling. *What in the world is going on?*

Suddenly, our hero's Choco-phone rings. He picks it up and answers, "Hello?" But before there's an answer, he notices the chocolate receiver is melting in his hand. With a mind as bright as a three-legged horny toad (latest research indicates horny toads are not terribly smart—no matter how many legs they have), our hero decides the only solution is to

Gobble, Gobble
Munch, Munch
Burp, Burp

eat the receiver.

But not to worry, dear reader. Thanks to some very clever writing on this author's part, a fax machine just happens to be sitting alongside the Choco-phone.

A moment later it rings and a fax starts printing.

Our hero grabs the fax paper, but instead of reading it, he uses it to wipe the Choco-phone chocolate off his hands! (Okay, so maybe he isn't as smart as a three-legged horny toad.) An e-mail message pops up on the computer screen, which also just happens to be sitting beside his fax machine. (Am I good or what?) Our hero turns to the screen and, since computer monitors are a lot harder to eat than telephone receivers, he begins to read:

> Greetings, Choco-Chump!¶
> By now you've discovered I'm replacing all of your favorite television shows with professional wrestling shows.¶

Chocolate Chum's mind spins. *Who could pull off such a dastardly deed? Who could possibly want to watch profes-sional wrestling, nonstop, twenty-four hours a day? And if he did, how could he possibly be smart enough to know how to send e-mail?*

He continues to read:

But it's not just your favorite shows, it's
everybody's TV shows!¶
And it's not just TV. My new, handy-dandy
Microwave Manipulator is changing all TV and
radio shows into wrestling matches. Soon
that's all anyone will be able to see or hear.¶

**"Oh no!" our delectable do-gooder
cries. "This can't be possible. Tell me
it isn't so!"**

It is so, Choco-*Chubs.* Soon the only
entertainment anyone will ever enjoy is
professional wrestling. Unless, of course,
you are foolish enough to try to stop me!¶

Slugs and kicks,¶
Outrageous Ray the Wrestler¶

P.S. Where's that bad-guy music that always
happens when bad guys talk in your stories?¶

TA-DA-DAAAA . . .

P.P.S. Thanks, that's more like it.¶

**Suddenly, our hero grows as pale as
a bar of white chocolate. And for good**

reason. The last time they met, Outrageous Ray held him in a hammerlock so long that he melted into a pathetic puddle of good-guy goo. It took months of physical therapy to shape him back into a respectable piece of milk chocolate.

And now...

The very thought makes him shiver, putting more bumps on his skin than the backside of a Nestle's Crunch bar. But a hero's got to do what a hero's got to do, so our hero does it. Without a moment's hesitation he goes to:

PLAN A

It's a complicated plan where he drops to his knees, starts wailing, and cries for his mommy. But when Mommy doesn't answer he goes to:

PLAN B

He leaps up, races to the Choco-Cave, hops in his Choco-mobile, and squeals out and onto the highway.

Precious seconds tick away. Who knows what damage Outrageous has already wreaked, what wreckage Ray has already reaped, not to mention the horrors of

seeing the entire Brady Bunch dressed
up as professional wrestlers! What—

Knock-knock-knock

I looked up.

"Wally, sweetheart, I've brought you your dinner . . . if you feel up to eating it."

It was Mom. I'd almost forgotten, I was supposed to be sick in bed!

"Just a minute," I cried.

The good news was my room is so small I could
leap to my bed in a flash. The bad news was my
room is so small that when Mom opened the door,
it blocked my path and I leaped into the back of
it instead.

K-THUD!

I staggered this way and that, that way and this
. . . seeing more stars than the Hollywood Walk of
Fame. Unfortunately, that was just the beginning
of my little catastrophe. In the next minute and
forty-seven seconds I was about to experience the
worst McDoogle mishap in the history of my life
. . . actually, in the history of the world . . . or what
would be left of it.

Chapter 2

The Cheating Begins

Actually, at first it didn't look like much of a disaster. In fact, on the McDoogle Scale of Mishaps it only registered about a 6.4. I mean, all I did was run face first into the door Mom had just opened . . . and stagger around a little, looking for a good place to fall.

"Wally, are you all righ—"

Unfortunately, the only place I could find to fall was into Mom.

"WALL—"

That was all she got out before I slammed into her. The good news was she managed to hang on to the tray with my dinner of tomato soup and macaroni and cheese. The bad news was that didn't stop us from staggering across the room and

K-Bamb!

slamming into the wall, where we accidentally turned on the switch to my ceiling fan. Unfortunately, our dance routine wasn't quite over. Next, we staggered over to my bookshelf and

K-Bamb!

crashed into my CD player.

No problem, except that Collision, the family cat (who did not get his name by accident), was sleeping on one of the speakers. Well, he had been sleeping on one of the speakers . . . until they blasted on and he shot straight up into the air . . . so high that he hit the ceiling fan and

MEOWRRR . . .
whip
MEOWRRR . . .
whip
MEOWRR . . .
whip

he hung on to the spinning blades for dear life as he flew around and around and around.

But even that wouldn't have been so bad if I hadn't managed to step on my skateboard and

"WHOAHHHH . . ."

send us both flying across the room toward Ol'
Betsy, which still sat running on my desk.
Fortunately, I veered us hard to the left and we
missed her. Unfortunately, we did not miss my
science fair project of cockroaches

K-RASH!
Tinkle, tinkle, tinkle
Scamper, scamper, scamper

The *K-RASH* was our hitting the glass terrarium. The *tinkle, tinkle, tinkle* was the glass
terrarium shattering. And, of course, the *scamper, scamper, scamper* was all those lovely cockroaches racing across my desk for freedom . . .
many of them across Ol' Betsy and some of them
straight into her keyboard.

Even that wouldn't have been so bad if Mom
didn't have like major "Cockroach*itis.*" It's a com-
mon disease among women that involves throwing up their hands and screaming for their lives
. . . not a great idea when those hands happen
to be holding a tray of tomato soup and macaroni and cheese. And an even worse idea if those
same food items should happen to fly high into
the air and hit a kamikaze kitty clinging to a
whirling ceiling fan, knocking him off and caus-
ing him to

K-SPLASH

fall smack-dab into my saltwater aquarium on the other side of Ol' Betsy.

Unfortunately, Collision liked water even less than Mom liked cockroaches, which meant

MEOWRRR . . .
K-RASH
chug-chug-chug

he panicked, dumped over the aquarium, and spilled water all over my desk.

The good news was the water helped wash most of the cockroaches out of Ol' Betsy's keyboard. The bad news was salt water (and a few confused fish) does even less than cockroaches to make computer keyboards happy . . . especially if it's accompanied by a

K-splash
glug-glug-glug

crashing bowl of tomato soup and

fling
K-splat
fling
K-splat

globs of macaroni and cheese flying off a whirling ceiling fan.

I looked down at my desk, horrified. Poor Betsy. She was popping and sizzling like bacon in a hot skillet . . . smoking and fuming worse than Dad trying to barbecue. Between the cockroaches, flopping fish, salt water, tomato soup, macaroni and cheese, and what looked like a little hairball Collision had thrown in for good measure, things did not look good for the ol' girl. Not good at all. Poor Betsy.

As I watched her, my heart sank. We'd written so many cool stories together. And now this. What a way to go.

"Oh, Wally," Mom said. "I'm so sorry."

"It's not your fault," I kinda croaked.

"Is there anything you can do?"

I shook my head and kept staring at the smoking and shorting-out circuits. It was hopeless. Any minute now she'd be heading for that great IBM factory in the sky. At least that's what I thought.

But luckily for her, I would be wrong.

Unluckily for me, it would have been more lucky if her luck had not been so lucky. Confused? Don't sweat it, it's all gonna start making sense in a minute . . . if you're lucky.

* * * * *

After carefully cleaning and wiping off Ol' Betsy (and retrieving what I hoped to be the last of the cockroaches from under her space bar), I said a silent prayer and turned her back on. To my amazement she still worked! It was incredible! A miracle! I turned on the Internet to check out the modem. It worked, too! I quickly brought my Choco Chum story to the screen, and it was in perfect shape, too! I couldn't believe it, everything was as good as new!

Unfortunately, better than new . . .

I first noticed something was up when I returned to my Choco Chum story and wrote something about our hero ordering a free case of chocolate bars from the local grocer for Choco's upcoming adventure. Fifteen minutes later, the grocer down the street knocked on the door and dropped off a case of chocolate bars . . . for free.

How weird.

Figuring it was just a coincidence, or a prize from one of those hundred and one contests Mom enters every week, I went back to the story and wrote how Choco Chum called up the local TV stations and ordered them off the air until he solved the Outrageous Ray Wrestling problem. Fifteen minutes later, my brothers were complaining that all of the TV stations in our city had gone off the air.

Uh-oh.

Next, as a test, I wrote that Choco Chum changed his mind and called up the stations to tell them to come back on the air.

Fifteen minutes later, all our stations were back on the air.

Double uh-oh.

That's when I decided it was time to invite Wall Street over. As a computer whiz who planned to make her first million by the age of fourteen, she played the stock market every lunch hour on the Internet. If anybody could figure out what was going on with Ol' Betsy, she could.

When she arrived, the first thing she did was run Ol' Betsy through about a hundred drills. When that was finished, she ran her through another hundred. Finally, she took off her glasses and rubbed her eyes.

"Well?" I asked.

"You're right," she said, "something's wrong."

"No kidding."

"I don't know how you did it," she sighed, "but you've got more fried circuits in there than Colonel Sanders has fried chicken."

"And?"

"And somehow you've created a program that— when Ol' Betsy is connected to the Internet— affects the real world."

"No way!" I cried.

"Oh, yeah. Big way. Somehow your program overrides all the other computer programs in the world and makes them think that what you type in your Choco Chum story is the actual reality."

"That's terrible!"

"Not exactly."

I could already see the wheels of commerce turning inside her head. I knew I shouldn't ask the next question, that it would only get me in trouble. But since there was no other village idiot around, I figured the job had once again fallen to the seasoned pro . . . me. "What do you mean . . . *'not exactly'*?" I asked.

Wall Street broke into her world-famous grin . . . the one she always grins before beginning one of her schemes. Without a word she turned back to Ol' Betsy and began typing.

"What are you doing?" I asked.

"I'm entering our school's computer," she said.

"You can't do that."

"I can't, but Choco Chum can."

"What?"

A moment later we were staring at Wall Street's upcoming report card. "Look at that," she whined. "Mrs. Fipplejerken is giving me a C in English again."

"Maybe if you tried studying," I suggested.

"Why bother studying?" There was that grin

again. Her fingers flew across the keyboard and she wrote:

**Choco Chum, change Wall Street's C
to a B.¶**

And, just like that, her grade changed to a B.

"That's amazing!" I cried.

"It sure is," she said, beaming. "The school computer believed that what we typed on Ol' Betsy was the truth, so it changed its information to fit."

"Wow," I said. "Okay, go ahead and change it back."

"Why?" she asked with the same grin.

"You can't keep it that way," I said.

"Why not?"

"Well, that's . . . that's cheating."

"No way."

"What would you call it?"

She thought for a second, then answered brightly, "Just knowing how to beat the system."

I frowned. "I don't think so."

"It's just one grade higher."

"Yeah, but—"

"Nobody's getting hurt."

"Yeah, but—" I seemed to be in a rut in the

debating department. Unfortunately, Wall Street wasn't. Suddenly, she had another idea.

"Here, check this out." Again her fingers flew over the keys until it was *my* report card up on the screen.

"Wall Street—"

"Take a look at that P.E. grade," she said. "See, right there. Kilroy is about to flunk you."

I stared at the screen. Sure enough, there was a big fat F glaring back at us.

"That really stinks," I complained. "Everyone knows Kilroy's got it in for me. That's so unfair."

"So let's make it a little more fair."

"What?"

Wall Street giggled and quickly typed:

Choco Chum, change Wally's F to an A.¶

Suddenly, the grade on the screen changed from an F to an A.

"Wall Street!" I cried.

"What?"

"That's . . . that's . . ."

". . . pretty cool, isn't it?"

I had to admit, it did look pretty cool seeing an A next to my name for P.E.

"Wall Street?" It was Mom calling from down-stairs. "Your mother's on the phone. She says it's time to come home."

"All right, Mrs. McDoogle," Wall Street called back. "Tell her I'm on my way." With that she reached over and started to shut down Ol' Betsy.

"Wait a minute," I protested. "You can't leave my grade like that."

Wall Street gave me one of her famous eye rolls . . . so hard I thought she was going to sprain them. "Wally, no one's going to care."

"Coach Kilroy will," I said. "He's been waiting all year to flunk me. Think how disappointed he's going to be."

Wall Street began to nod. "Good point."

It was about time I had one. I let out a sigh of gratitude. Then, without a word, she reached down to Ol' Betsy and typed:

Choco Chum, make sure Coach Kilroy no longer teaches at our school.¶

"Wall Str—" But before I could stop her she snapped the computer off. "Wall Street?!"

"What?" she said, looking at me with that grin.

I stared at her, unsure what to say. Part of me

wanted to order her to turn Ol' Betsy on again and change my grade back to an F. But another part of me sure liked the idea of that A. Then there was the thing with Coach Kilroy. It would sure be cool if for some reason he was transferred to another school, where he couldn't torment me. But still . . .

"Come on," Wall Street urged. "Let's keep it, just for a day, and see if anything happens. We can always change it back if we want to."

I looked from her, to the computer, then back to her again. And then, for some unknown reason, I felt my head begin to nod up and down.

"Great," she said, gathering her things and heading for the door. "I'll see you tomorrow." And, just like that, she was gone.

I sat there for a long moment . . . feeling kind of bad and kind of excited at the same time. Of course, I figured it was just a computer glitch and everything would be back to normal in the morning. Unfortunately, my figurer had misfigured this figure.

Translation: Things were going to get majorly weird majorly soon . . .

Chapter 3

Bye-Bye, Kilroy

"Tuck and roll, McDoogle!"

TWEET!

"Tuck and roll! Tuck and roll!"

It was another grueling day of Coach Kilroy's extra credit class, and he was busy doing what he did best—yelling at and humiliating me. (Actually, he was just doing the yelling, I took care of the humiliating part.)

Since I'd pretty well destroyed the obstacle course the day before, we met inside. Now he had us running around on tumbling mats, holding tightly wrapped gym towels. Every time he blew his whistle, we were to pull the towel into our gut and tumble, doing our best not to crush it.

"When that massive food shortage hits," he

screamed, "and you're the only one with a loaf of bread within twenty miles, you gotta protect it with your very life!"

TWEET!

"Tuck and roll! Tuck and roll!"

Actually, I was doing a pretty good job of running and pretending to hold the imaginary loaf of bread in my hands. I was even falling down all right (I'd had lots of practice). It was only when I *tucked* just a little too close to the door and *rolled* just a little bit out into the hallway that things got just a little bit ugly. Actually, it wasn't even the tucking and rolling, but the bouncing down the flight of stairs . . .

> *bounce*— "Ouch!"
> *bounce*— "Ooch!"
> *bounce*— "Eech!"

that got painful.

"McDoogle, you moron!"

Of course, everyone had a good laugh. Everyone but me . . . and Wall Street, who rushed down to the bottom of the steps to help me up. Normally, I'd be embarrassed getting helped by a girl, but when you're majorly unconscious and seriously considering death as a pastime, you forget those minor details.

"Too bad that computer thing didn't work," I groaned as she helped me sit up and we started counting my broken bones.

"Actually, it did," she said.

"What?"

"I called up Mrs. Fipplejerken this morning and asked her if I could do extra credit, kind of like we're doing here, to raise my grade."

"And?"

"She said I was already getting a B . . . just like we typed in Ol' Betsy."

"No way," I said.

"Big way."

"But what about Coach Kilroy. How come—"

Suddenly, I was interrupted by a loud police siren. Actually, several loud police sirens. I got up and kinda half limped, half dragged myself to the nearest doorway to take a look. By the time I stepped outside, there were about a hundred policemen swarming around the building, and they were all heading in one direction . . . straight toward the gym doors.

"All right, Kilroy!" a police officer shouted through a blow horn. "Come out with your hands up."

"What's going on?" I whispered to Wall Street.

She shook her head. "I don't think we really want to know."

A moment later, Coach Kilroy stepped outside. His hands were on top of his head, and he looked even more clueless than me. "What's going on?" he shouted. "What have I—"

But that was all he got out before a half-dozen officers jumped him and tackled him to the steps. Coach shouted, officers yelled, kids screamed.

"What's happening?" I cried to Wall Street.

She said nothing as we watched them hoist Coach to his feet and cuff his hands behind his back.

"What's going on?" I yelled.

Slowly Wall Street turned to me. Her usual grin was no longer grinning. And for good reason. "Looks like Ol' Betsy kicked in after all," she said.

"Huh?"

"It looks like we really are getting rid of Coach Kilroy . . . for good."

* * * * *

Wall Street and I burst through the front door of my house and headed for the stairs. Opera was right behind.

"Sweetheart," Mom called as we breezed past her. "I just heard the news. Isn't that a shame about Coach Kilroy?"

"Yeah," I shouted as we raced up the steps to my room.

"Such a pity," she said, shaking her head. "To think that nice man actually robbed seventeen banks."

Suddenly, we came to a screeching halt. Well, two of us came to a screeching halt. With Opera's extra weight, it took a little longer for him to slow down, which explains why

THUD, THUD
CRUSH, CRUSH
SUFFOCATE, SUFFOCATE

I was suddenly on the bottom of a giant, two-man pig pile.

"Opera," I gasped. "I . . . can't . . . breathe . . ."

"Oh, sorry," he said as he staggered back to his feet.

Wall Street and I pulled ourselves back up and, after checking for any major injuries, we turned to Mom. "What did you say?" I asked.

"I just saw it on the news," she said. "There's some confusion about the fingerprints and surveillance tapes, but they're pretty sure he's the one who's been holding up all of those banks."

I looked at Wall Street and Opera. They looked at me. Then we turned and raced up the stairs for all we were worth. We entered my room, and I quickly turned on Ol' Betsy. As she booted up, Opera kept shaking his head. "I can't believe it, I can't believe it, I can't believe it."

"Believe it," Wall Street said as she grabbed a chair and scooted behind me. "Whatever we type on Ol' Betsy actually happens."

"That's right," I said as I brought the Choco Chum story up on the screen.

"See"—Wall Street pointed—"right there it says, *'Choco Chum, make sure Coach Kilroy no longer teaches at our school.'*"

"That's the last thing we typed," I said.

"Only we didn't fill in the details, so Ol' Betsy's fried circuits did it instead," Wall Street said.

"By getting Coach arrested?" Opera asked.

"Exactly. Ol' Betsy contacted whatever computers were necessary to make that come true, and those computers changed their data to make it a reality."

Opera seemed to be getting it . . . although he obviously had something else on his mind as well. "So, you mean if you were to type something in like, oh, I don't know . . . , *'Opera gets a giant dump truck load of Chippy Chipper Potato Chips . . . ,'* then that would happen?"

Wall Street nodded. "The computers would make it become a reality. Go ahead, show him, Wally."

"Guys," I said, "I really don't think we want to keep messing with—"

"Go ahead," Wall Street insisted. "It won't hurt anything."

I turned to her. "Don't you think we've done enough—"

Before I could stop her, she reached past me to the keyboard. "Honestly, Wally, sometimes you can be such a chicken." I watched as she typed:

Choco Chum, deliver a dump truck full of potato chips to Opera.¶

"That's it?" Opera asked. "That's all you do?"

"Yup."

"Are you sure? Because I don't feel like anything has changed."

"Of course you don't feel anything," Wall Street sighed. "Unless you're a dump truck or a load of potato chips, you wouldn't. But just be patient, they'll show up."

"Cool. Maybe you could order me a couple of double-decker cheeseburgers with—"

"Guys," I complained, "we're supposed to be clearing up the problem with Coach Kilroy, not creating new ones."

"So go ahead," Wall Street said, scooting back and letting me get to the keyboard. "Clear it up."

It took a moment to decide what to type. Obviously, there was a major mix-up in the computers about Coach Kilroy and the fingerprints and the video surveillance tapes and everything. So, I finally reached for the keys and typed:

Choco Chum, clear up all of the confusion about Coach Kilroy.¶

"There," I said. "That should do it."

Wall Street nodded. "Things should be getting back to normal in no time."

I looked back to the screen, pleased that for the first time in history I had actually ended a major McDoogle mishap before it had grown out of hand. Incredible.

Little did I realize how incredibly wrong I was.

Chapter 4
Uh-Oh

After Wall Street and Opera left for home I tried to relax a little. Normally, I would have whipped out my computer and unwound by writing my superhero story. But I was still a little nervous about Ol' Betsy's fried circuits, so I grabbed a tablet and a pencil and went to work the old-fashioned way . . .

When we last left Choco Chum, he was not changing Wall Street's and Wally's grades, and he was definitely not getting rid of any middle school P.E. teachers (particularly any whose names start with Coach and end in Kilroy).

(Even though I was only writing this on paper, I figured better safe than sorry.)

Instead, our stupendous and sometimes
sticky (but only when he sits in the sun)
superhero sits in his Choco-mobile racing
toward Outrageous Ray the Wrestler's secret
hideout. (I'd like to tell you where it is, but
it's a secret.)

No one's sure what made Outrageous Ray so
outrageous. Some say he just liked neon green
tights, flamboyant capes, and shoving his
finger at ugly opponents, screaming, "I want
you! I want you! I want you!" Then there
is the ever-popular theory that Ray really
wanted to be president, but found politics
far too rude and violent for his tastes.

Whatever the reason, Outrageous soon became
the most famous (and outrageous) wrestler in
the world. I mean, the guy ate, drank, and
slept wrestling. Now it looked like he wanted
to eat, drink, sleep, and watch it on every
TV channel as well.

As Choco Chum squeals around the last
corner and pulls up to Ray's hideout at Mold's
Gym. . . . (Oops, now you know its location.
Well, at least I didn't tell you it was the one

in Cleveland. Oh, there I go again. But at least
I didn't mention it's at 3427 Rutledge Drive.)

Anyway, as he squeals around the corner to
the now not-so-secret hideout, he slams on his
brakes and gasps a good-guy gasp. For there,
across the street in the J. C. Nickel's display
window (it used to be J. C. Penney's, but you
know how inflation is), a hundred TV sets are
tuned to a hundred different stations...each
showing a hundred different professional
wrestlers sharing their most intimate feelings:
"And after I rip your arm off, I'm going to
rip off your other arm, and then rip off your
other arm, and then..." (Listen, I know they
said "arm" three times, but these guys are
athletes, not mathematicians.)

Still, their lack of math skills is not the
problem. The problem is the dozens of
impressionable kiddies standing outside the
display window staring up at the screens, all
wanting to be just like these guys (as soon as
they can find an opponent with three arms).

Without a moment's hesitation, Choco Chum
leaps out of the car, races up the steps to Mold's

Gym, and throws open the doors: "Outrageous
Ray," he shouts. "Outrageous, where are you?"

Suddenly, our hero is hit by blinding beams
of light. The beams are coming from all sides.
He shades his eyes and sees it's the reflection of
the sun off a dozen wrestling championship
belt buckles—each brighter and more gaudy
than the next. But that's only the beginning
of Choco Chum's concerns. For the longer the
sunlight shines, the hotter he becomes. And
the hotter he becomes (you guessed it), the
more he begins to melt.

Suddenly, he hears a sickeningly sinister
snicker: "Moo-who-ha-ha-hee-hee..." (the
type of snicker taught at bad-guy schools
everywhere), and he knows it can only come
from one place:

(insert bad-guy music here)

"Outrageous!" our hero cries. "Is that you?"
"Moo-who-ha-ha-hee-hee..."
The laughter makes Choco Chum shudder
with fear. But this is no time for cold feet. In
fact, as he glances at his tootsies, he detects

that they're turning just a tiny trace too toasty. (Say that seven times fast.) Don't get me wrong, there's nothing bad about having warm feet…unless, of course, those feet happen to be made out of 100 percent pure milk chocolate. Because, as any chocolate creatures will tell you, if their feet get too warm they soon come down with a dreaded case of…puddle paws.

The beams grow hotter.

"Outrageous…"

A voice booms from behind the light of the belt buckles. "I've always said you were an old softy," it shouts. "Now you're proving my point!"

Our hero glances at his knees. They are weakening and also turning into goo…then his waist…then his chest…then his face…

"Outwaggouus!" he cries. "Com ou inn thhh opp…ennn…" But that's all our heroic hero can holler. (It's hard hollering anything when your mouth is melting.)

Great Scot! What can our little puddle of dude goo do? Will he ever be able to pull himself together? And, more important, is he really 100 percent pure milk chocolate

or did they mess him up by putting in those
stupid nuts or fruit or crispy rice thingies?

"Wally . . ."
I tried to ignore the voice and kept on writing.

And then, just when all is lost—

"Wally, come on downstairs!" It was Mom.
"They're talking about Coach Kilroy on TV again.
You won't believe what's happening now!"
I paused for a second and looked at my story.
It was getting pretty weird. But even as I looked
at it, I feared Choco Chum's little fantasy was
nothing compared to Coach Kilroy's great big
reality . . .

* * * * *

I raced down the stairs doing my usual crash-
and-burn routine. You know, the one where my
feet kinda get tangled in the carpet at the top of
the stairs and I kinda

Crash, Crash, Crash

tumble down the steps (making sure to catch each one on the way down) until I hit the lamp at the bottom, breaking it into a bazillion pieces.

Of course, Dad was already there ready to help me up. Poor guy. All he wants is for me to be a real man like my superjock brothers, Burt and Brock. But before he has a chance to say anything, Mom shouts, "Hurry up, guys. The police chief is talking about Coach Kilroy."

"The police chief?" I cried as I limped into the room.

"Shh." She motioned for me to be quiet as I joined the rest of the family, who were already watching the show. Sure enough, there was Police Chief O'Brien holding a news conference. Camera lights were flashing, videotapes were running, and Chief O'Brien was talking.

"By enhancing all of the video images and fingerprints, we are now positive that Mr. Kilroy is indeed the perpetrator of all seventeen bank robberies."

"What?" I cried.

"Shhh . . ." Mom and Dad both motioned for me to be quiet. "And by running a computer check, we've discovered another remarkable fact: Mr. Kilroy's fingerprints and video image are an identical match to every unsolved crime in our city for the past five years."

"That's not true!" I shouted.

"Shhhhhhh . . ." Now everyone in the family was giving me the leaky tire routine.

"But, Ol' Betsy is—"

"Wally!" they all cried.

The chief continued, "We are as surprised as anyone that all of these crimes have suddenly been cleared up, but the evidence is crystal clear. One man, and one man only, is responsible . . . Coach Morton Kilroy."

The reporters began shouting a bunch of questions, but I barely heard them. I was still in a daze when the phone rang and Mom answered. A moment later, she called out to me, "Wally? Wally, it's one of your little friends."

I don't know how I managed, but somehow I shuffled over to the phone and answered, "Hello?"

"Did you *munch munch* hear the news?" I could tell it was Opera by the perpetual crunching in my ear.

"Yeah . . ."

"There's *crunch crunch* more."

"More?" I croaked.

"Yeah, we've got to *crunch munch* have a meeting. Wall Street's on her way over here now. You've got to *munch crunch* come, too. And bring Ol' Betsy."

"Why? What's up?"

"Just get over here as fast as you *BURP* can. It's worse than you can *BELCH* believe. I gotta go!"

"Opera . . . Opera!" No answer. He'd hung up.

I returned the phone to its cradle. Because of his perpetual munching, I knew something was wrong. Normally, Opera eats a little junk food most of the time, but when he's really nervous he eats *a lot* of junk food *all* of the time. And by the way he was scarfing down those empty carbos, I knew we were in for some major, big-time trouble.

Chapter 5

Uh-Oh x 2

I knew things had gotten weirder the moment I saw the mound in Opera's driveway. From a distance I couldn't exactly make out what it was, but I didn't have to. The sound gave it away:

Crunch, Crunch, Crunch
Crunch, Crunch, Crunch
Crunch, Crunch, Crunch

Then, of course, there was the smell. Nothing comes close to the delicately scented aroma of extra crispy, extra extra salty, extra extra extra greasy *Chippy Chipper Potato Chips*—the chips preferred by heart surgeons around the world (who are looking for more bypass operations to perform).

When I got close enough to see the details, it was exactly as I feared. There in the middle of the driveway was a giant mound of potato chips.

And there, at the top of that mound, happily eating his way down to the bottom, was my ol' pal Opera.

"Opera!" I shouted. "Opera, what's going on?"

Munch, Munch, Munch
Munch, Munch, Munch
Munch, Munch, Munch

"Opera!"

"He can't hear you."

I spun around to see Wall Street standing in the front doorway.

"What happened?" I asked. "What's all this about?"

"Remember the last thing we typed on Ol' Betsy about Choco Chum ordering a dump truck load of chips?"

I felt a huge knot growing in my stomach. "Yeah . . ."

"There they are."

I glanced back at Opera as he sat atop the golden pile of chips, slowly, but surely, eating his way down toward us.

"How do we get him off there?" I asked.

"Got it covered," she said. "I just had to find something he liked better than chips."

"What could he love better than chips?" I asked.

She grinned and produced a giant tub of *Greas-o* (the cooking grease preferred by those same heart surgeons everywhere). Without a word, she grabbed a pile of chips from the mound and shouted, "Hey, Opera!"

He looked down just long enough to see her dipping the chips into the tub of lard.

"Umm . . . ," she shouted, pretending to lick her lips. "Yum, yum, yum."

He scampered down the mound in a flash as Wall Street held out the grease-dipped chips, urging him to follow her into the house . . . "Come on, boy, attaboy, come on."

He trotted obediently behind her. I followed. Once we got inside, she tossed him the chips, and he gobbled them down while she quickly locked the door—making his escape impossible.

"Okay," she said, turning to me, "we've got a problem."

"No kidding."

"Opera," she asked, "are you sure your parents won't be home until late?"

He looked up from his eating and answered, *"Burp!"*

"Great, then we'll make this headquarters."

"Headquarters for what?" I asked.

"Turn on Ol' Betsy, plug her into that kitchen phone line there, and let's get to work."

"What are you talking about?" I demanded as I set up the computer and plugged in the phone line. "We typed out that Choco Chum would make everything okay with Coach Kilroy, and just the opposite happened."

"Not exactly," she said. "Bring the story up on the screen."

Reluctantly, I turned on the computer and brought up our last Choco Chum command:

Choco Chum, clear up all of the confusion about Coach Kilroy.¶

"See!" I pointed to the screen. "It's right there."

Wall Street shook her head. "No."

"What are you talking about? It's right there in front of you."

Again she shook her head. "We typed in the command for all of the confusion to be cleared up."

"And?"

"And it has. Ol' Betsy decided to clear up the confusion by making it one hundred percent clear that Coach Kilroy was guilty."

"What?"

"We typed in that Choco Chum should clear up the confusion about Coach Kilroy. That's exactly

what happened. There's no more confusion. Ol'
Betsy cleared it up by making Coach look completely guilty."

I could only stare at the screen and groan. "This
is terrible."

"Tell me about it."

"So what do we do?" I asked.

"We gotta go down to the jail and clear it up."

"No way," I cried. "They're not going to listen to
a bunch of kids."

"You're right," Wall Street said.

"BELCH!" Opera agreed.

"So what do we do?" I demanded.

"Just give me a second," Wall Street answered.

Opera and I exchanged uneasy glances. Of the
three of us, Wall Street was definitely the brains.
Unfortunately, her brains often involved our
bruises. Still, we were the ones responsible for
this mess, and we were the ones that had to do
some—

"I got it!" she shouted. "You say they won't listen to a bunch of kids, right?"

Opera and I both nodded. "Right."

"But what if we were more than just kids? What
if the three of us held important offices?"

"What do you mean?" I asked nervously.

"Here, I'll show you." She moved in front of the
screen and started typing:

Choco Chum, make Wally the new police chief.¶

"What!?" I shouted.

"If you're the police chief then you can get every-body to listen you. You might even be able to get Coach out of jail."

"That's loony tunes!" I cried. "No way am I going to the city jail all by myself and pretend to be the police chief."

Wall Street saw my point and began to nod. "You're right," she agreed, "you shouldn't have to go in there by yourself." She reached back to the keyboard and typed:

Choco Chum, make Wall Street the police chief's secretary and . . .¶

She paused to think for a moment (which made me even more nervous) until her face suddenly lit up:

. . . make Opera the jail's new dietitian!¶

"What's that?" Opera asked.

"You know," she said, "like a cook."

"Wall Street," I protested, "don't be ridicu—"

But that was all I got out before she reached down and hit "ENTER."

I stared at Ol' Betsy helplessly. There must have been a hundred things I wanted to say all at the same time. Unfortunately, the only thing that came out was the tried-and-true:

"Uh-oh . . ."

Opera nodded, belched, and added, "Times two."

* * * * *

The next day was New Year's Eve. Since the following day was a holiday—and since Coach Kilroy wasn't around—his survival workshop had been canceled. This fit in perfectly with Wall Street's plan . . . something about three very frightened kids putting on their best clothes, heading down to the city jail, and pretending to be the police chief, his secretary, and the new jail dietitian. Of course, it would never work (the only thing more dangerous than my clumsiness was Wall Street's plans), but we had to do something.

"This is crazy," I mumbled for the hundredth time as we got off the bus and headed up the courthouse steps.

"You worry too much," Wall Street said as we entered the doors. "Just keep Ol' Betsy there nice and handy in case we get into trouble."

I nodded as I pulled Ol' Betsy a little closer under my arm.

"Where are the snack machines?" Opera asked as we stepped into the lobby. (Hey, everybody's got their priorities.)

Up ahead was a guard sitting behind a security window. I leaned over to Wall Street and whispered, "He'll never let us in."

"Just go past like you know what you're doing."

"But . . ."

"Don't worry," Wall Street said. "Ol' Betsy hasn't let us down yet. If Choco Chum says you're the new police chief, then you're the new police chief."

"But . . . but . . ."

"And don't forget Coach Kilroy. The poor guy is totally innocent."

"But . . . but . . . but . . ."

So there I was, doing my motorboat imitation until the guard behind the window asked, "You kids want something?"

He looked at me. My palms grew damp.

He looked harder. My forehead grew wet.

He looked even harder. Perspiration streamed down my face. Talk about police brutality. If I sweated any more they'd mistake me for an indoor fountain.

Fortunately, Wall Street came to my rescue. "Police Chief McDoogle reporting for his first day of work," she said in her deepest, most grown-up voice.

The guard gave us a slight smile. "Right."

"I'm serious," Wall Street said. "This is Chief McDoogle, I'm his secretary, and this here is the jail's new cook."

The slight smile grew to a slight grin.

"I'm not joking," Wall Street insisted. "If you don't believe us, just check the records."

"Why don't you children run along now and play somewhere else."

"If you would just—"

"Go on now, before I lose my patience."

Suddenly, with the world's biggest scowl, Wall Street turned to me and said, "Chief McDoogle, I suggest you take down this man's badge number and immediately put him on report."

The guard's smile drooped slightly. Wall Street turned back to him. "The chief's a merciful man. If you'll just look at your records, I'm sure he'll go easy on you."

With a heavy sigh the guard reached for the computer keyboard. "Look, kiddies," he said as he began to type. "I don't know what sort of game you're playing, but—" Suddenly, he stopped. "That's funny."

Wall Street and I exchanged glances.

He looked up at me. "What's the name again?"

And always being the quick thinker that I am, I responded, "Uh . . . duh . . . hmm . . ."

"McDoogle," Wall Street said. (I told you she was the smart one.) "Wally McDoogle."

He stared at the screen, hit a few more keys, and shook his head in amazement.

Wall Street and I fidgeted nervously.

Finally, he spoke. "I don't understand it, but . . . you're right. It says right here, 'Police Chief Wally McDoogle.' Now when did that happen?"

"It was sort of a last-minute appointment," Wall Street said.

"But you're just kids."

Wall Street motioned toward the monitor. "Computers don't lie."

He glanced back to the screen, hit a few more keys, and nodded. Then he looked back at me and asked, "You got any I.D.?"

Since my last answer worked so well, I tried it again. "Uh . . . duh . . . hmm . . ."

Once again, Wall Street came to my rescue. "I.D.?" she asked.

"Yeah, you know, something to prove he's"—he

looked back at the screen—"*Wally McDoogle.*
Maybe a passport, or a driver's license, anything."

My mind raced a thousand miles an hour. The
only problem was it raced a thousand miles an
hour in circles, which is the same as racing
nowhere at all. It seemed no matter how hard I
tried, I just kept coming back to the same tried-
and-true answer: "Uh . . . duh . . . hmm . . ."

"Is that really necessary?" Wall Street asked.

The guard nodded. "Just because he says he's
Wally McDoogle doesn't mean he's—"

Suddenly, I had it. "My milk ticket!" I blurted
out.

Everyone just sort of stared at me. Well, everyone but Wall Street, who was already shaking her
head in silent wonder at my stupidity.

"No, I'm serious," I said as I pulled the school
cafeteria milk ticket out of my pocket. "It's got my
signature and everything." I held the beat-up piece
of paper to the glass for the guard. "See . . . right
there, 'Wally McDoogle.'"

He carefully scrutinized it. "What are all those
red drops on it?" he asked. "They look like blood."

"Oh"—I grinned—"that's where I accidentally
stabbed myself with a ballpoint pen."

"He's never been good with pointy objects," Wall
Street explained.

The guard could only stare at it. Then he stared at the computer screen. Then he stared at me. My heart was pounding so hard I was afraid he could hear it. Then, shaking his head, he reached for a button. The door buzzed, and we pushed it open. A moment later, all three of us were inside the city jailhouse.

"The offices are on the third floor . . . *Chief McDoogle.* I'll be calling up there to have someone meet you and straighten this out."

"Thank you," I croaked. And then, wanting to sound more official, I added, "You can bet there'll be a big promotion in this for you."

Before the guard could answer, Wall Street grabbed me by the arm and pulled me toward the elevator. "Don't overdo it," she whispered.

"Overdo it?" I asked. "You just had us break into the city jail pretending to be public officials, and you tell *me* not to overdo it!"

"Let's hurry!" Opera said as he pushed the elevator button. (Having spotted no vending machines it was obvious he wanted to get to the third floor, to see if his luck was any better.)

How had it happened? How, by using Ol' Betsy to cheat just a little, had we gotten into such a jam? Unfortunately, I was already beginning to understand that cheating is a lot like lying. The Bible makes it pretty clear that there's no such thing as a "little lie" (if you don't believe me, check out *My Life As Dinosaur Dental Floss*). The same is true with a little cheating. Cheating is cheating. And, just like lying, it's wrong in a major uh-oh, I-guess-I-won't-be-trying-that-again kind of way.

"Wall Street?" I croaked.

"Yeah?"

"Now what do we do?"

"What we've always done," she said as the elevator doors finally opened and we stepped inside.

"What's that?"

She waited until the doors closed and we were trapped inside before giving her answer; one I could have lived another millennium without hearing: "We fake it."

Chapter 6

Faking It

Once we were outside the police chief's office, his secretary stopped us. The good news was that the real police chief was at some fancy breakfast making some fancy New Year's speech with a bunch of fancy people. The bad news was that Wall Street had actually managed to talk his secretary into *not* throwing us out.

"Just look at your computer," Wall Street kept saying. "Just look at your computer."

When the woman finally did look at the computer, she scowled hard at her screen. "It must be some sort of glitch," she said. "There must be a bug in our system."

"Then check out the other systems," Wall Street said. "Check the mayor's system. Check the governor's. Check every computer in the state! They'll all say the same thing: Wally McDoogle is the new chief of police!"

"Well, I'll just do that, young lady," the secretary said.

And when she did, she was even more surprised. It was exactly as Wall Street had predicted. Every single computer gave the same information: Wally McDoogle was the new police chief . . . Wall Street was his new secretary . . . and Opera was the new dietitian. Although she wasn't happy about the situation, the secretary agreed to give us a spare office and let Opera go down to the kitchen— at least until she sorted things out. That was her plan.

Unfortunately, ours would be a little different.

While I sat back to survey my office, Wall Street left to start her detective work. A few minutes later she barged into my new office with a stack of papers just slightly taller than the World Trade Center. As she plopped them down on my desk, I asked, "What are these?"

"They're the forms you need to sign so Coach Kilroy can go free."

"I can't do that!"

"Of course you can. You're the police chief, remember?"

I shook my head. "Wall Street, we've got to stop this. We've got to tell them this is all a lie. We've got to tell them there's some mixed-up microchip in my computer and that we—"

"You're going to tell Coach Kilroy that *you're* the reason he got arrested?"

"Well, uh . . ."

"That *you* manufactured all that evidence against him?"

"Uh . . . duh . . ." I was back to using my brilliant debating skills again.

"That *you're* the reason he's in jail?"

"Uh . . . duh . . . hmm . . ."

"And then," she continued, "when everything's all cleared up, and you finally get out of prison for impersonating an officer, you're going to go back to finish P.E. and face whatever torture Coach Kilroy has been planning for you all that time?"

I looked at her.

She looked at me.

And then, taking my famous McDoogle stand for courage, I grabbed the pen and asked, "Where do I sign?" But I'd barely written my name on the paper when an alarm sounded.

"What's that?!" I shouted.

"I don't know!" Wall Street yelled.

We raced out into the hallway to join the secretary. "What's going on?" I cried.

"The prisoners are rioting!" the secretary shouted.

"Why?"

"For lunch somebody cooked them a greasy

potato chip casserole smothered in salt and topped with even greasier corn chips!"

My suspicions rose.

"That's disgusting!" Wall Street shouted over the alarm.

"Actually," the secretary yelled, "it's the two inches of *Greas-o* poured over each helping that really upset them."

My suspicions were confirmed. "Where exactly are the jail cells?" I yelled.

"Behind those steel doors at the end of the hall!" the secretary shouted.

Without a moment's hesitation, I turned and started down the hallway.

"Wally," Wall Street yelled. "Where are you headed?"

"Enough is enough!" I shouted as I continued forward. "I'm not sure how, but I'm going to clear this up once and for all!"

"Not by going in there, you're not!"

But I'd made up my mind. Maybe it was the hope of getting to talk to Coach Kilroy. Maybe it was explaining to the inmates the real problem. I didn't know. All I knew was that it was time to start being honest.

I arrived at the steel doors. To my right, a guard sat in a room with thick glass walls where he could see both our hallway to his left and the jail cells to the right. I gave him a nod, but he hesitated.

I cleared my voice and shouted over the alarm, "As police chief, I'm ordering you to open this door."

He looked nervous.

I tried again. "Mister, that is a direct order from your superior officer!" I wasn't sure it would work, but it always did the trick in those army movies. I figured I'd give it a try. He threw a nervous look at the secretary, who reluctantly nodded. Finally, he reached down and pressed a button.

The steel door clicked loudly and then swung open.

"Wally!" Wall Street shouted. "Don't go in there! Wally, that's crazy!"

Crazy?! I thought. *Crazy* is when you accidentally create a mixed-up microchip and start using it to cheat with your grades. *Crazy* is when you have to cover that cheating by having your coach arrested. *Crazy* is when the only way to free him is to pretend you're the chief of police. If you want to talk crazy, then *that's* crazy!

I stepped through one doorway and then the other until I was finally in the hall where all the jail cells were. That's when I realized Wall Street's definition of crazy might be better than mine after all.

The place had gone berserk. Prisoners were

yelling and banging on the bars of their cells. Some were flinging Opera's gourmet masterpiece in every possible direction including

K-Splat

mine. A kitchen worker had started a grease fire, and the place was filling up with more smoke than our house when it's my little sister Carrie's night to cook.

But it wasn't just the food that was making them so angry. Someone had also gotten hold of the overhead PA and was playing Pavarotti or Tortellini or one of those Italian opera guys. It was terrible. Almost as bad as Dad's solos in the shower. And there was only one person to blame.

"Opera!" I shouted as I stumbled through the smoke-filled hall. "Opera, if you can hear me, turn that stuff off! Opera!"

There was no answer . . . at least not from Opera. There was, however, another voice I recognized.

"McDoogle! McDoogle, is that you?"

I spun around to see a man with his face pressed against the bars. It might have been Coach, but I couldn't be sure. I mean, without his sweats, his whistle, and his constant shouting at me, it was hard to tell, until he finally shouted:

"McDoogle, you moron, what are you doing here?"

Yup, that was him.

"McDoogle!"

"I'm here to get you out."

"What?"

Without another word I turned back to the guard in the glass booth and shouted, "Unlock this man's cell."

The guard looked confused and uncertain.

"I said, unlock this man's cell!"

"McDoogle," Coach yelled, "what are you doing?"

I gave no answer. "Guard! As police chief, I am giving you a direct order. Unlock this cell, now!"

With as much enthusiasm as someone getting a tetanus shot, the guard finally obeyed and hit the button. Immediately, Coach's cell door unlocked. I pulled it open.

"McDoogle, what are you—"

"I'm rescuing you!" I shouted over all the noise. "Hurry!"

Reluctantly, he stepped out of his cell to join me. We turned and headed back toward the guard, who pressed another button. The steel door swung open, Coach and I stepped through, and a moment later we entered the office hallway.

"Wally!" Wall Street shouted. "Coach Kilroy!"

But that was as far as our little reunion went.

Because at that exact instant the real police chief
stepped out of the elevator with Opera. He took a
look at me, then he took a look at Coach Kilroy.

"All right, McDoogle," Coach half-whispered.
"Tell me what we're supposed to do now."

I sized up the situation and quickly put my
McDoogle genius to work. I evaluated every pos-
sibility and every consideration until I finally had
a plan.

"Well?" Coach demanded.

I opened my mouth and at the top of my lungs
suggested the best idea I'd had all day:

"RUN!!!!"

Chapter 7

11:59 and Counting . . .

Since the real police chief was busy blocking the elevator, and since running seemed to be our only option (either that or suddenly admitting everything, which would be far too easy and end all of this pain, misery, and misadventure), we decided to head for the stairs. I took the lead (a definite mistake for all involved), Coach Kilroy followed, then Wall Street and Opera.

I reached the door to the stairs, threw it open, and we started down them.

"Wally!" Wall Street shouted from behind me.

But I couldn't be bothered. I was on a mission. I'd gotten us into this mess, and now it was up to me to get us out.

"Wally!" she repeated.

"Don't worry!" I shouted over my shoulder. "I'll get us down to the exit!"

"Wally!!"

"What!"

"If we want to go downstairs, why are we heading up the stairs?"

I came to a stop. (The only thing worse than my lack of coordination is my lack of direction.) "Sorry," I said, starting to turn back, "I guess I wasn't thinking."

Suddenly, Coach Kilroy held out his hand and stopped me. "Then we're doing the right thing?"

I looked at Wall Street. She looked at me. I looked at Opera. He looked at me. Then in perfect three-part harmony we all turned to Coach and looked at him: "Huh?"

He explained. "Every time McDoogle thinks, he gets into trouble. Right?"

"Right." We all nodded.

"No offense," he said, "but he ain't the brightest bulb in the pack. Right?"

"Right," we agreed.

"Or the most athletic," Opera offered.

"Or the best looking," Wall Street agreed.

"Or the most gracefu—"

"All right, all right," I said, "I get the point." I looked at Coach and asked, "So what do *you* suggest we do?"

He answered, "You've thought it over and want to go down, right?"

"Right."

"Then we better hurry and go *up*."

Of course. It made perfect sense. Without a word, I turned, and we continued running up the stairs—me doing what I do best: wearing myself out, coughing and gasping for breath, and Coach doing what he does best: "Come on, McDoogle! Move it! Move it! Move it!"

And then, just when I was about to sprain a lung, we reached the door to the roof. I pushed against it with all my mightiness, which we've already established is pretty mighti*less,* but the door didn't budge.

"Come on, McDoogle, push!"

I leaned back and slammed my body into it as hard as I could.

K-Bamb

The door still didn't move.
Coach continued yelling, "McDoogle!"
I hit it again, even harder.

K-Bamb!

Still no door movement, still more Coach yelling: "McDoogle!!!"

Suddenly, Wall Street had a brainstorm. She reached past me and turned the knob. The door

opened effortlessly. (Hey, I'm a writer, not an engi-
neer; I can't be expected to know how everything
works.)

Sunlight poured over us as we raced out onto
the roof.

"There!" Coach spotted a fire escape on the other
side of the building. "Over there!"

We all took off. After my usual staggering and
stumbling across the roof, including the mandatory running into a few air-conditioning vents
along the way, we finally made it to the fire escape.
This time Wall Street suggested I go last. I didn't
understand why until everybody got down to the
street and it was my turn. Suddenly, the reason
became crystal clear. Because once everybody else
was down, it made my landing

> *K-Bounce . . .*
> *K-Boink . . .*
> *K-Break . . .*

> *K-*"OOAF!"

a lot easier. Well, easier on me. I'm not so sure
about those I landed on.

We circled around the back of the building, but
we didn't dare go out to the main street. Because
there, in front of city hall, stood a bazillion police-

men and SWAT team members. Of course, I recognized most of them from my past McDoogle mishaps. And, of course, I wanted to step out and say "hi"—you know, talk about old times, see recent photos of their kids and stuff.

But Wall Street held me back. "You can't go out there," she whispered. "They'll arrest you for sure."

I nodded.

"And we can't go home, 'cause they've probably already got our places surrounded."

Again I nodded.

"So what do we do?" Opera whined. It had been several minutes since he'd had any junk food, and it was obvious he was starting to go through withdrawal.

Wall Street shook her head. "I don't know."

"I do," Coach said.

We all turned to him. "Remember how I've been telling you kids to prepare for the big computer crash? How when that Y2K bug hits tonight—*New Year's Eve*—that there's going to be rioting in the streets?"

We all kinda rolled our eyes. How could we forget? That's all Coach had lived and breathed these last few months.

"Well, preparing is exactly what I've been doing," he said. "In fact, I've made sure the underground bunker in my backyard has enough food and water

to last for months. Let's hide out there. Come on!"
He turned and started toward his house.

I threw a nervous glance at my buddies. Don't
get me wrong, I appreciated the offer, but being
cooped up in an underground bunker with Coach
Kilroy wasn't exactly my idea of a good time. Then
again, being his prison cellmate for the next
twenty years sounded even worse. Reluctantly, I
turned and followed. So did Wall Street, and,
finally, Opera—not of course without asking,
"Excuse me, Coach, but exactly how big is your
supply of dehydrated chips?"

* * * * *

To make sure we wouldn't be noticed, Coach
kept us in the back alleys and shadows until nightfall. Then, to be certain no one was tailing us, he
had us zig and zag through the streets for hours
until he was sure it was safe to head for the
bunker. As far as I could tell, it was pretty much
a waste of time. Everybody was so excited about
their big Millennium New Year's Eve parties that
they really didn't pay any attention to us. But that
didn't stop Coach. In fact, by the time we'd finally
zigged our last zig and zagged our last zag, it was
almost midnight.

At last we arrived. Coach pulled open the big metal door, and we climbed down inside. As far as dirty, cold holes in the ground went, the bunker wasn't half bad (if you happen to like dirty, cold holes in the ground).

Of course, Coach thought it was great. In fact, all he did was keep telling us how lucky we were. "Yes, sir, this is a terrific place to hide," he said. "Not only that, but when the clock strikes twelve and all the computers in the world crash, you'll thank your lucky stars you're safe in here with me, instead of out on the streets with them rioters."

"You really believe things are *crunch, crunch, crunch* going to get crazy at midnight?" Opera asked, while munching on the dried cucumber chips he'd found. (Hey, desperate times call for desperate junk food.)

"Believe it?" Coach practically shouted. "I know it!" He looked at his watch. "In just two minutes and thirty-seven seconds, when all the computers crash, civilization as we know it will cease to exist!" He went on jabbering about some sort of computer bug that would throw everything into chaos, but Wall Street and I weren't paying much attention. Instead, we'd found Coach's phone line in the bunker, plugged in Ol' Betsy, turned her on, and tried to figure out what to do next.

"There's only one thing we can do," Wall Street finally said.

"Delete the program and hope everything just magically turns back to normal?" I asked.

"Don't be ridiculous," she said scornfully.

(Hey, it was worth a try.)

"No, we have to give you more clout," she said. "Instead of police chief, we have to make you someone more powerful. Someone who can actually pardon the coach."

I swallowed hard. "You mean like the mayor?"

Wall Street shook her head. "No, the mayor's not powerful enough to do that . . . only the—" Suddenly, her eyes lit up like a Christmas tree. "Actually, only the governor can pardon people."

"The governor!"

"One more minute, kids," Coach shouted. "One more minute before the New Year comes and the destruction of society begins."

I barely heard. I was too focused on Wall Street. "You can't be serious," I said.

"It's the only way. Here"—she reached for Ol' Betsy—"let me have that." Before I could stop her she typed:

Choco Chum, turn Wally into the state's governor.¶

"Wall Street!"

She hit "ENTER."

"What have you done?" I cried. "That's crazy!"

"Why do you say that, Mister Governor?"

"Mister Governor? Stop that, I am not the—"

"Stop what, sir?"

"Thirty seconds," Coach called.

"Wall Street, you've got to put an end to all of this, right now!"

"Sir, I'm not the one with the mixed-up computer that tells all the other computers in the world what to believe. Nor am I the one responsible for all of this mess."

She was right, of course. I glanced down at Ol' Betsy. I don't know what had gotten into her (other than all the salt water, the fish, those half-dozen cockroaches . . .). But, whatever it was, it was definitely the cause of our troubles. (Well, that, and the minor fact that we'd been trying to cheat.)

"Fifteen seconds!" Coach shouted.

"Listen," I said. "Enough is enough."

"What do you suggest we do, Mister Governor?"

"Stop calling me that!"

"Ten seconds."

"Here." I nudged her away from Ol' Betsy and stared at the screen. There had to be some way to stop all the craziness . . . some way to wipe the slate clean and get everything back to normal.

"Five seconds!"

Suddenly, I had it! I reached for the keyboard and started typing.

"Four . . ."

Choco Chum, clear up all the computer messes by—¶

"Three . . ."

—wiping their slates clean!¶

"Two . . ."

"No!" Wall Street shouted. "Wally, not that!"

But I'd made up my mind. Before she could stop me I reached over and—

"One . . ."

—hit "ENTER."

Suddenly, there was a squeal of brakes outside, followed by a loud crash, and then a scream.

"What's that?" Opera cried.

"And so it's begun," Coach answered grimly.

"What?" Opera shouted. "What's begun?"

There was another crash and another scream
. . . and then another . . . and another.

"What's going on?!" I shouted. "People are getting hurt. We've got to go out there and help them!"

Before Coach could grab me, I squeezed past him and raced up the steps to the bunker's door.

"Don't!" he yelled. "There's nothing we can do!"

"Of course there is," I shouted as I pushed open the door. "We've got to help!"

"McDoogle—"

But he was too late. I'd pushed open the door and stepped outside. There was more squealing of brakes, more crashes, and more screaming. I scampered out of the bunker and raced toward the back fence to see what was happening.

When I arrived I could only stare in horror. Just beyond the fence was something that looked like a combination war zone and demolition derby. All of the traffic lights were out and car after car was crashing into one another. Up above, the transformers on the light poles were blowing up and sending showers of sparks over everyone. And the people . . . everywhere they were running, shouting, screaming. It was terrible, everyone was out of control, it was almost as bad as the Day After Christmas Sale at the mall!

Wall Street was the first to arrive at my side.

"Nice work, sir."

"I don't understand," I said. "What happened?"

She handed me Ol' Betsy. "Take a look at your screen. Look at what you typed."

I glanced down at the screen and read:

Choco Chum, clear up all the computer messes by wiping their slates clean.¶

"I still don't understand," I said, straining to hear her above the sounds of screaming, chaos, and crashing cars.

"You've fulfilled Coach's prediction. You've 'wiped everything clean.'"

A fire engine roared past with its siren blasting, and I had to shout. "What?"

"I said, you've wiped everything clean!" she yelled.

"How?"

"You and Ol' Betsy have just cleared every bit of memory from every computer in the world!"

"That's impossible!" I shouted.

She pointed to all of the chaos going on in front of us. "See for yourself." By now, dozens of cars were piled up and more were flying past. Fire hydrants were sheared off, spewing water high into the sky. Across the street, people were breaking into a local grocery store, stealing food. And there was no longer any light except for the cascading sparks from the exploding transformers.

"I don't get it!" I shouted. "What's going on?"

By now, Coach was beside us. As he surveyed the scene, he answered quietly, "It's only the beginning."

"The beginning of what?" I yelled.

"The beginning of the end of the world."

Chapter 8

The United States of Wally

The good news was my house was only a few blocks away. The bad news was a few blocks was like a few light-years—at least with all the craziness going on around us. Still, I had to get home. I had to see if my family was okay.

Convincing Opera to leave with me wasn't too hard.

"Your folks got *BURP* chips?" he asked.

"You bet," I said.

He glanced at the empty bag of cucumber chips in his hands. "Nothing weird like spinach chips or broccoli chips or some sicko health thing like that?"

"No way," I said. "We've got the real thing—complete with grease, salt and . . . and . . . and more grease!"

"All right!" He gave me a high-five. "So, what are we *BELCH* waiting for?"

83

Wall Street wasn't quite so easy to convince. "I don't know," she said. "What about Coach?"

"Yeah," Coach agreed. "It's gonna get lonesome spending twenty-four hours a day doing sit-ups, push-ups, pull-ups, chin-ups, fifty-yard sprints, and squat-thrusts all by myself."

Suddenly, Wall Street was a little more sure about leaving.

"Besides," Coach continued, "who am I going to yell at and chew out if you're all gone?"

Suddenly, Wall Street was a lot more sure about leaving. So was I.

After bidding a fond farewell to Coach (and promising he could call up and yell any time he got too lonely), we hopped over the fence and started running down the street through the chaos to my house.

Things were getting worse by the minute. By now, nearly every store had been broken into. Everywhere people were stealing and looting. Men were fighting over kerosene lanterns. Women were fighting over bread. Children were fighting over old Barney toys! (I told you it was bad.)

I wanted to shout to them and explain that it was all a mistake, just another McDoogle Mishap. But after Wall Street pointed out that it might lead to an uncomfortable situation (like my death), I decided it was best to keep my mouth shut and my feet moving.

When we finally got to my place, I was glad to see my family staying cool and calm. The generator was working, and Dad was pouring what water had been left in the pipes into jugs to be placed with the rest of our supplies; and little sister Carrie was helping Mom gather candles. The only people having major panic attacks were Burt and Brock, my twin superjock brothers:

"We're going to miss tomorrow's bowl games," they kept screaming. "We're going to miss the bowl games!" I was clueless about which bowl games they were talking about (Rose Bowl, Orange Bowl, Tidy Bowl—They're all the same to me). The point is: everyone else in my family was staying calm. Although not as fanatical as Coach, Dad had always said we should be prepared for something like this, and for the most part we were.

When we were sure we weren't needed, Wall Street, Opera, and I raced upstairs to my room. Whatever Ol' Betsy and I had done, it was important to undo it as soon as possible. But how?

We quickly turned on my computer and plugged it into the phone line, hoping it still worked. Sure enough it did. But the screen had no sooner come up than a message began flashing across it:

> URGENT
> URGENT
> URGENT

"What's going on?" Wall Street asked.

"I don't know," I said.

"It must be another computer glitch."

"I don't think so," I said. "It didn't come on the screen until we plugged into the phone line."

"How can it work? Everything's been wiped clean—even the phone lines!"

"I don't know!"

Suddenly, there was a long, loud

BEEP

followed by more letters. All three of us leaned forward to read the screen as the words quickly formed:

TO: GOVERNOR WALLY McDOOGLE¶
FROM: THE PRESIDENT OF THE UNITED
          STATES¶

I gasped. Wall Street gasped. Opera gasped. Then, looking for something else to do, we decided to keep reading.

WE HAVE ISOLATED THE GLOBAL CHAOS
TO THIS LOCATION. YOU HAVE EXACTLY

TEN MINUTES TO CEASE YOUR
AGGRESSION. IF YOU DO NOT CEASE AND
DESIST, WE WILL CONSIDER YOUR ACTIONS
AN ACT OF WAR UPON THE UNITED
STATES OF AMERICA AND WE WILL
RESPOND SWIFTLY AND APPROPRIATELY.
THIS IS YOUR FINAL WARNING, GOVERNOR.
I REPEAT, THIS IS YOUR FINAL WARNING.¶

HAVE A NICE DAY,¶
THE PRES.¶

All three of us stared at the screen a good minute.
Finally, Opera asked a question that wasn't exactly
on any of our minds: "I thought you said your parents had chips."

I ignored him and turned to Wall Street. "If all
the phone lines are down, how can the President
e-mail us?"

She shrugged. "I guess when it comes to national
emergencies, he's got ways."

"But what does he mean when he says they'll
respond *'swiftly and appropriately'*?"

Wall Street took a deep breath and slowly
answered. "I think the *swiftly* part means he'll be
declaring war on us."

I slowly nodded. "And the *appropriately* part?"

"It means they'll be bombing us to smithereens."

I let out a long, low sigh and mumbled, "I just hate it when this type of stuff happens."

* * * * *

As usual, Wall Street and I had like the longest debate over what to do. She wanted to keep trying to fix things by using Ol' Betsy's powers, and I just wanted to call it quits.

"Look," I said, "this whole thing started by trying to cheat with our grades."

"Which are still," Wall Street happily pointed out, "what we changed them to."

"What difference does that make now?!" I shouted.

"I'm just trying to look on the bright side."

"The bright side? The bright side!? The President of the United States is about to declare war on my house, and you want me to look on the bright side?!"

"Actually," Opera said as he began looking under my pillow, "I don't think the President can legally do that."

"Why not?" I asked.

Now he was checking between my blankets. "To declare war on a foreign country, I think he has to get Congress to vote on it or something."

"We're not a foreign country," I said. Now he dropped to his knees and stuck his head under my bed. "Opera, what are you doing?"

"Don't you ever like eat popcorn and chips and stuff in bed?" he asked as he started rummaging around underneath. "You musta dropped crumbs around here somewhere. I mean everybody drops—ah, here we go."

crunch . . . crunch . . . crunch

Even though it was faint, I could still hear the muffled munching of Opera finding something to eat under my bed.

"Hold it," Wall Street said. "He might have something."

"Of course, he has something," I said. "Probably a stray corn chip or pretzel left over from—"

"No, no, no," Wall Street said as she rose to her feet and crossed back to Ol' Betsy. "I mean about declaring war on us. If we're a foreign country, maybe the President can't declare war on us without getting Congress's permission by a majority vote!"

"But we're *not* a foreign country," I repeated.

"Not yet," she said with a twinkle in her eyes. Once again she reached for Ol' Betsy.

"Wall Street!" I was on my feet racing toward

her. But by the time I arrived, she'd already finished. I looked down at the screen and stared in disbelief:

Choco Chum, make Wally's home a separate country.¶

"Oh, no!" I groaned.

"Don't take it so hard," Wall Street said. "Instead of a governor, you're now the President of an entire country."

I buried my face in my hands. "No, no, no, no . . ."

But even as I spoke, Wall Street had gone back to her typing. I no longer had the courage to look, and when she finished I could only mumble, "What is it now?"

She was just about to answer when, suddenly, there was a huge

ROAR . . .
whooooosh

followed by another, and another, and another.

"What's that?" I cried as I raced to my window for a look.

I wished I hadn't. Because there—at the far end

of my street—were a bunch of jet fighters coming in low and fast.

"We're under attack!" I cried. "They're about to bomb us!"

"No way!" Wall Street shouted.

"Yes, way!" I cried.

She shook her head and started to answer but it was impossible to hear over another sound that began pounding the air.

Whop, whop, whop, whop . . .

I craned my neck to look up through the window and saw a half-dozen helicopters dropping down from the sky.

"And helicopters!" I cried. "They're attacking with helicopters, too!"

"This is not an attack," Wall Street shouted over the noise.

"What?!"

"This is not an attack!" She started for the door. "They haven't had time to declare war on us."

"Then what is it?" I shouted.

"Follow me."

"What?"

"Come on, I'll show you!" And with that she was gone.

Reluctantly, I followed. I threw a glance at Opera.

His feet were still under the bed. I figured I'd leave him alone. After all, everyone's entitled to a last meal.

By the time I got down the stairs, Wall Street had opened the front door and was heading outside to join my family.

K-WHOOSH
K-WHOOSH
K-WHOOSH

As I approached the doorway, I saw that the jets weren't flying overhead to bomb us; instead, they were landing on the street in front of us!

K-WHOOSH
K-WHOOSH
K-WHOOSH

"What on earth . . . ?" I said to myself.

When I finally stepped outside, it was even crazier. The helicopters were

WHOP, WHOP, WHOP, WHOP

landing in my front yard.

I'd barely joined Wall Street and my family when the door to the first helicopter slid open and out stepped a general-type guy with a gazillion medals on his chest. He quickly walked toward us, scanning each of us up and down. "Which one of you is Wally McDoogle?" he barked.

My family, being the loving, supportive type they are, all stepped back and pointed. "He is!"

The General turned and marched straight toward me.

I knew it was over. I knew it was curtains. I knew I had better straighten out my cheating problem with God before I met Him face-to-face . . . because, by the looks of things, that meeting was about to happen.

"President McDoogle?" the General shouted. He raised his hand . . . probably to beat me or shoot me or whatever they do to foreign dictators.

I closed my eyes and nodded, expecting the worst.

"General Pending reporting as ordered, sir."

I opened my eyes. The General was saluting me. "Wh-at?" I asked.

"General Patton Pending with the troops you requested, sir."

I cut a look at Wall Street, who was grinning ear to ear. "What did you write on Ol' Betsy?" I asked. "What's Choco Chum done now?"

She said nothing.

"Wall Street?"

Her grin grew bigger.

"Wall Street!"

And bigger some more.

"Wall Street, answer me!"

Finally she spoke, but I wished she hadn't. "What good is it being president of a country," she said, "if you don't have an army to defend that country?"

Chapter 9

This Means War!

"Wall Street!" I cried.

"Don't worry"—she grinned—"the General and I, we've got it covered."

"Got it covered?" I yelled. "Got it covered! The United States of America is about to declare war on us, and you've got it covered?!"

"Sir, please . . ." The General crossed to my side and lowered his voice. "As commander in chief, it's important that you don't let the troops think you're panicking."

"But I *am* panicking!"

"Listen"—he glanced from side to side then back to me—"if you just leave everything to me, I guarantee it will all work out."

I held his gaze. He did his best to crank up a smile, but it came out as more of a grimace.

"How can you be so sure?" I asked.

"Trust me"—(more of his grimace smile)—"I'm a professional."

"Well . . ." I took a deep, uneasy breath. "I don't know what other choice we have, so I guess it might be okay if—"

Before I could finish, he spun around and shouted, "All right, men, secure this house and make it headquarters."

Suddenly, a hundred soldiers leaped out of the helicopters and raced toward our house.

"Now, hold it just a minute!" Dad shouted. He held out his hands, trying to stop them. "You can't just land in the middle of our front yard and expect—"

"Immobilize him!" the General barked.

Instantly, a dozen soldiers threw Dad to the ground, slammed a dozen booted feet on top of his chest, and pointed a dozen rifles at him.

"On second thought"—Dad nervously cleared his throat—"please make yourselves at home."

"Release him!" the General ordered. Then, as the soldiers obeyed and turned to race up the steps, the General kneeled down to Dad and whispered, "I'll be keeping a special eye on you, mister."

"General . . . Mister General?" I raced up to him.

He spun around. "Yes, sir?"

"You say you're going to fix things. How exactly are you going to do that?"

"Well, sir, it's rather complicated. I'm sure someone in your position wouldn't be interested in—"

"Try him," Mom said as she joined me.

The General gave her a stern look, but she held his glare and wouldn't back down. When he finally realized who he was up against (nobody crosses Mom and gets away with it), he turned and looked over the neighborhood . . . a neighborhood where people were exiting their houses and running for safety as fast as possible. "War is a game," he said overdramatically. "And, like any other game, there are certain rules, certain guidelines, certain principles . . ."

"Meaning?" Mom asked.

"Meaning . . ." He turned back to her and continued, "The best defense is always an offense." With those simple words, he turned and started up the steps.

"But . . ." I raced to his side. "What does that have to do with the United States declaring war on us?"

He sighed wearily and slowed to a stop. "What it means is, the only way to defend ourselves from the U.S. declaring war on us . . . is to declare war on them first."

"What?"

Like a gentle father, he reached down and patted me on the shoulder. "Don't worry about a thing, sir. We'll take care of the details."

"Details!?"

Suddenly, loud grating sounds echoed up and

down the street. We spun around to see all the manhole covers on the road being lifted up from below. A moment later frogmen in wet suits and scuba gear began climbing out.

"Ah, good." The General smiled. "The navy's finally here."

"The navy?" I cried.

"Yes, it was a bit difficult for them since the nearest ocean is two thousand miles away, but they have a great fleet of submarines, and you have a great sewer system. Now, if you'll excuse me, sir, I have a war to win." With that he turned and entered the house.

"Wallace!" It was Dad. To say he was in a lousy mood might be an understatement. To say he was so mad he was about to blow a heart gasket . . . well, you'd be getting close.

"Yes?" I asked, giving him my best wide-eyed, innocent routine.

But, before he could respond there was a low

rumble, rumble, rumble,

that quickly grew to a loud

RUMBLE, RUMBLE, RUMBLE.

"Now what?" I moaned.

The good news was that I didn't have to wait forever to find out. The bad news was that even forever wasn't long enough. Because coming down both ends of our street were dozens of giant tanks. But they weren't only coming down the street. They were also busting through:

CRUNCH, CRUNCH, CRUNCH

the fence of our backyard, and

SMASH, SMASH, SMASH

through the neighbor's house across the street.

"Great," I groaned, "now we've got tanks for our little army."

Wall Street came to my side. "Actually—"

"Haven't we seen enough?" I interrupted.

"Actually, uh—"

"I mean, how many more weapons do we need?"

"Actually, uh, Wally . . ."

"What?" I finally turned to her.

"Those aren't *our* tanks."

"They're not?"

"Nope."

"Then whose are they?"

"Guessing by the American flags, I'd say they might be American."

I slowly turned back to the tanks. As if on cue, they all began grinding to a halt. A moment later there was only silence.

So there we stood in my front yard, completely surrounded by tanks, completely frozen in fear. That is, until each of the giant guns on those giant tanks swiveled toward us, bringing us into their sights.

"Say, Wall Street?"

"Yes, Wally?"

"You wouldn't happen to have any suggestions, would you?"

"Not really."

"Are you certain?"

"Well, maybe just one."

"I see. And what might that be?"

"Actually, it is not my best, I mean, I have had better."

"I understand," I said.

"And I really haven't had much time to think it through."

"I can appreciate that," I said. "But given this particular situation, in our particular time frame, what in particular would you suggest?"

"Something we've had a lot of experience at."

"I see." I nodded. "Please continue."

"First, I suggest we turn around like so."

I followed her example. "Okay, good."

"Then I suggest we take a deep breath."
"All right." I took in a deep breath. "Now what?"
"Well, now, I suggest we

"RUNNNNN!"

You'd think by now I'd have gotten tired of following Wall Street's suggestions. But, considering the options (her way, or death's way), this one didn't sound half bad. So the two of us ran up the porch steps as fast as we could. Any second I expected those giant guns to open fire, any second I expected to be turned into a little pile of McDoogle dust. But nothing happened. Nothing at all. Well, unless you count the part where Wall Street opened the door and I

K-Bamb

ran into the edge of it.
"Come on, Wally!" she cried as I began my typical stumble-and-fall routine. "Quit clowning around."
I nodded, doing my best to stay on my feet as I staggered back toward the door and

K-Bamb

ran into it the second time.

By now, I'd been on the porch just slightly longer than forever, and I couldn't figure out why they hadn't already opened fire on me until

K-Bamb

I hit the door the third time. That's when I heard the snickers coming from the direction of the tanks, then the laughter, then the out-and-out knee-slapping guffaws. It was a great comfort to know I was entertaining the troops (it would have been an even greater comfort if they had been *my* troops—but I suppose you should spread goodwill wherever you can).

Finally, Wall Street grabbed me by the collar and yanked me through the doorway. Once inside, she cried, "Are you all right?"

"Yeah." I nodded, still dazed from all the door *K-Bamb*ing. "I wonder why they didn't shoot me."

"Must have thought you were on a suicide mission," Wall Street said as she examined the three giant bumps on my forehead.

By now, my vision had pretty much stopped blurring, at least long enough to see what they'd done to the house. I suppose it wasn't too bad . . . if you don't mind a few walls knocked down to make room for the machine guns, or that the kitchen was now being renovated into a missile launching center. Then, of course, there were the trenches and foxholes being dug in the living room. (War can be a real hazard to carpet sometimes.)

"Wall Street . . ." I slowly turned to her.

"I'm thinking," she said. "I'm thinking, I'm thinking . . ."

Knowing that she was thinking brought little comfort, although I appreciated the effort.

"*BURP.*"

I spun around to see Opera coming out of the back bedroom. "Hey, these rations aren't *BELCH* half bad."

"What are you eating now?" Wall Street sighed.

"Spam chips." He grinned.

Her expression made it clear she was sorry she'd asked.

"Mister President?"

I turned to see the General motioning for me to join him at the front window. (Well, it had been a front window—now, with the glass smashed out, it was more like a front opening.) "We've reestablished the electricity and utilities for this quadrant, sir." He held out a pair of night vision goggles. "Would you like to survey the troops, sir?"

I walked over to join him. "Did you see those tanks outside?" I asked.

"No problem, sir."

"Did you see all those guns pointed at the house?"

"No problem, sir."

Suddenly, a half-dozen red laser beams poured into the room, filling it with a half-dozen bright red circles.

"What's that!?" I cried.

"That might be a problem."

Before he could explain, the phone rang and a nearby soldier picked it up. "Hello?" he said. Then, with a trembling hand, he held it out to me. "It's for you, sir."

"Who is it?" I asked. Unfortunately, I didn't have to wait long to find out."

"President McDoogle?" the voice on the other end asked.

"Uh, this is Wally McDoogle, yes."

"This is the President of the United States. How are you doing today?"

"Um . . . not real good, sir."

"Oh, sorry to hear that. Well, listen, do you happen to see a bunch of bright red laser dots filling your room there?"

I glanced around. "About half a dozen," I said.

"Ah, excellent."

"What are they?"

"Well, they're part of our laser-guided bomb system."

"Your what?"

"We have about, oh, I don't know, a hundred

or so bombers circling your city. Each has several of those fancy laser-guided bombs, which, coincidentally enough, all happen to be aimed at your house."

"A hundred bombers!" I choked.

"Give or take a dozen. Anyway, before they drop their bombs, you have about thirty seconds or so if you'd like to make any last requests."

I opened my mouth then closed it. Then opened my mouth and closed it. I suppose I could have stood there doing my fish imitation the rest of my life, which by the looks of things wouldn't be all that long, but I had to think of something and it had to be fast.

Chapter 10

Wrapping Up

"Thirty seconds . . ." That's all the President of the United States said we had left before we were bombed to smithereens! I glanced at my watch. Better make that 29 seconds. Er, 28. The point is that we were running out of time. Without a moment's hesitation, I dropped the phone and raced for the stairs.

"Mister President!" the General shouted after me.

"Wally!" Wall Street yelled.

"BURP!" Opera cried.

But this was no time to talk. It was time to do what I should have done when I had time to do what I should have done when I had time to do it.

Translation: No more cheating or trying to fix the cheat.

I arrived at the stairs, taking them two at a time, which (thanks to my athletic ability) only meant spraining both ankles . . . twice. But it didn't matter. It was time for the truth.

I glanced at my watch: 22 seconds and counting.

I arrived at my bedroom, which now served as a lookout post.

19 seconds.

There on my desk was Ol' Betsy, looking just as innocent as she always did. And why not? It wasn't her fault I'd gotten us into this mess.

17 seconds.

"Excuse me," I said, squeezing past a bunch of soldiers with binoculars, telescopes, and listening devices, "excuse me, please, excuse me," until, finally, I reached Ol' Betsy.

"Wally!" Wall Street arrived outside my door, shouting. "What are you going to do?"

I glanced at my watch:

14 seconds.

"What I should have done at the beginning," I yelled. I picked up my computer, started unwinding the extra-long phone cord connecting her to the wall, and headed for the door. "I'm putting an end to Ol' Betsy!"

"You're what?" she cried as I squeezed past her and into the hallway.

I didn't answer but headed down the hall toward the bathroom. I suspected Dad had filled the tub and sink to store more drinking water, but if I did this right, all of our problems would be over in a few seconds. If I didn't do it right, *we'd* be over in a few seconds. Speaking of which . . .

10 seconds to go . . .

Wall Street stayed at my heels, arguing all the way. "If you destroy Ol' Betsy, you'll destroy your Choco Chum story! You'll destroy all of our hard work . . ."

I turned and entered the bathroom.

8 seconds . . .

Wall Street continued. "You'll wind up getting that F in P.E."

I nodded. Now at last we were getting close to the truth.

". . . and I'll, I'll, I'll wind up getting a C in English instead of a B!"

We were even closer.

6 seconds.

I arrived at the tub. It was full. With shaky hands I held Ol' Betsy over it. The water was deep and clear . . . and it would spell instant death for her.

"Wally! There has to be another way!"

I couldn't think of any. I had to destroy the computer bug. I had to destroy Ol' Betsy.

4 seconds.

"Delete!" Wall Street shouted. "Hit the delete button! It will erase all of your Choco Chum story!

It will erase everything we've ever written for him to do."

3 seconds . . .

I looked at her. I looked at Ol' Betsy. Maybe she *was* right, maybe there *was* another way. Maybe I could spare Ol' Betsy's life and still straighten everything out. Maybe all I had to do *was* to delete the Choco Chum story.

2 seconds . . .

"Wally, you've got to believe me! Just hit 'DELETE'!"

I reached for the delete key, my finger hovering over it.

1 second . . .

"Wally, do it! Hit the delete key! Now! Hit it now!"

Finally, I pressed it.

Ol' Betsy started churning and grinding away, making more noise than Dad's stomach in church when he's had too many pieces of anchovy pizza the night before. It was pretty obvious, the old girl didn't want to give up the program. But she kept on grinding until finally, after a couple of last-minute grunts and a few more groans, the most amazing thing happened . . .

A single cockroach scurried out from under the keypad. He glanced around kind of dazed and confused. He looked up at me, gave his antennae a little rub, then hopped off the keyboard and into the tub, landing with the tiniest splash. After a dozen backstrokes he made it to the edge of the tub, crawled up the side, and disappeared into a crack in the molding.

"That was it!" Wall Street cried. "That's what was wrong with Ol' Betsy. That's what was scrambling up her program. She really did have a computer bug!"

I hoped Wall Street was right, but I couldn't be certain, not yet. I stuffed Ol' Betsy under my arm and headed back into the hallway. Out there, soldiers were standing around, scratching their heads, looking confused and trying to figure out what had happened.

I headed for the stairs. Down below the General was still shouting out orders, but they were a different type. "All right, men, I want this place shipshape and clean as a whistle—and I mean now!"

As I arrived, he spotted me and walked over. "Sorry, kid," he said. "I'm not sure what all happened." He let out a long sigh and continued. "Best we figure, it was that Millennium Bug. Messed up everybody's computers—the government's, the military's, everyone's."

I slowly nodded.

"Not to worry, though," he said. "Looks like some genius has just solved it. Before you know it, everything will be back to normal."

I nodded again.

"Oh, here," he said, handing me the phone. "It's the President. He still wants to talk to you."

I took it in shaking hands and numbly answered, "Hello?"

"Wally? Wally McDoogle?"

"Yes, sir?"

"Listen, sorry about the little mix-up. Best we figure it was that Millennium Bug thing."

"Yes, sir."

"Anyway, I trust there are no hard feelings. Tell your folks we'll get the house and everything else fixed up lickety-split."

"Yes, sir."

"Oh, and Wally."

"Sir?"

"To help express our sincere apology and to prove there are no hard feelings . . ."

"Sir?"

"Well, tell your friend, Opera, that there will be no charge for all those Spam chips he's eaten."

"Thank you, sir," I said. And then, ever so slowly, I hung up.

* * * * *

It only took a few days for things to get cleared up. Eventually, the power came back on, stores got food back in, and people finally started to relax. Of course, everybody had their theories about what had happened. But only Opera, Wall Street, and I knew what had really gone on and what the real "computer bug" was. And now that everything was all fixed up, we figured why bother explaining. After all, what they didn't know wouldn't hurt us.

When school finally began, Coach Kilroy was back, doing what he did best . . . flunking me and shouting, "Come on, McDoogle, move it, move it, move it!" Opera returned to having to buy his own potato chips. And Wall Street, well, Wall Street was already dreaming up another plan to make her millions . . . something about selling original pieces of Noah's Ark (the fact that they were plastic and made in Hong Kong didn't seem to slow her down any). Good old Wall Street.

I, on the other hand, had decided to return to writing my superhero story. Chocolate Chum was history, he'd always be history; just typing his name made me nervous. But that was okay 'cause I'd already dreamed up a replacement. So late the following evening, I opened up Ol' Betsy and once again started . . .

It has been another super swell day for the stunningly stupendous and superb

superhero...Lemon Lad. Already he has
talked a restaurant chain into replacing all their maple syrup with lemon
juice (ever try waffles smothered in
lemon juice?...Don't!), convinced a local
broccoli farm to start selling broccoli
pickled in lemon juice (Double Don't!),
and broken up a half-dozen Lemon Lovers
Anonymous meetings by standing up and
shouting, "Hi, my name's Lemon Lad, I'm
a Lemonaholic...AND I'M PROUD OF IT!"

Now, with the satisfaction that he has
again made the world a tastier, tarter,
and just a little bit tangier place to
live, our hero pops out his microwave
meal of spaghetti and lemon balls
(smothered in extra lemon juice), and
heads on over to turn on the TV.

But instead of his favorite game
show, *Wheel of Lemons,* there's a bunch
of crazed overweight guys yelling and
jabbing their fingers at each other.
"Oh, brother," our hero groans, "it's
another political debate"...until he
realizes these guys aren't politicians,
but professional wrestlers.

He switches channels.

But it's the same thing. Instead of

Touched by a Lemon Drop, it's another
wrestling match.

He switches again. Now, instead of
that famous lemon wedge singing, "I love
you, you love me," there's even more
wrestling.

I hesitated a second and stared at the screen.
It looked like we were off to a pretty good start.
Only this time my hero wouldn't get sidetracked
with any urge to cheat. Neither would I. Truth is,
I planned never to cheat again. Call it learning
another one of life's little lessons. The point is, it
doesn't make any difference how small the cheat
is, or how secretive you think you're being . . . one
way or another, it will always come back and get
you. Always.

I was about to resume typing when I noticed
the slightest movement against the far wall . . .
the wall next to the bathroom where my little
cockroach buddy had disappeared. Without a
word, I reached into my desk drawer, pulled out
a can of Raid, and continued typing.

Yes, sir, life is full of lots of lessons. Including,
of course, the old motto . . . always be prepared.

You'll want to read them all.

THE INCREDIBLE WORLDS OF
WALLY McDOOGLE

#1—My Life As a Smashed Burrito with Extra Hot Sauce
When Wally is forced to stand up to Camp Wahkah Wahkah's bad guy, it's one hilarious mishap after another . . . until he learns the importance of loving your enemy. (ISBN 0-8499-3402-8)

#2—My Life As Alien Monster Bait
A movie company has chosen Wally to be eaten by their mechanical "Mutant from Mars!" But which will consume Wally first—the disaster-plagued special effects "monster" or his own out-of-control pride? (ISBN 0-8499-3403-6)

#3—My Life As a Broken Bungee Cord
A hot-air balloon race! What could be more fun? Until calamity builds on calamity and with his life on the line, Wally learns how to FULLY put his trust in God. (ISBN 0-8499-3404-4)

#4—My Life As Crocodile Junk Food
Wally visits missionary friends in the South American rain forest. Here he stumbles into a whole new set of impossible predicaments . . . until he understands the need and joy of sharing Jesus Christ with others. (ISBN 0-8499-3405-2)

#5—My Life As Dinosaur Dental Floss
Wally learns the importance of telling the truth as he is pursued by a SWAT team, a TV news reporter, bungling terrorists, photo-snapping tourists, and Gary the Gorilla. (ISBN 0-8499-3537-7)

#6—My Life As a Torpedo Test Target
When Wally uncovers the mysterious secrets of a sunken submarine, his dreams of fame and glory soon turn to hostile sea creatures, pirates, and a war against his own greed and selfishness. It isn't until Wally finds himself on a wild ride atop a misguided torpedo that he realizes the source of true greatness.
(ISBN 0-8499-3538-5)

#7—My Life As a Human Hockey Puck
Jealousy and envy drive Wally from one calamity to another until, as the team's mascot, he learns the importance of humility while suddenly being thrown in to play goalie for the Middletown Super Chickens!
(ISBN 0-8499-3601-2)

#8—My Life As an Afterthought Astronaut
"Just 'cause I didn't follow the rules doesn't make it my fault that the Space Shuttle almost crashed. . . ." So begins another hilarious Wally McDoogle MISadventure as our boy blunder stows aboard the Space Shuttle and learns the importance of: Obeying the Rules! (ISBN 0-8499-3602-0)

#9—My Life As Reindeer Road Kill
Santa on an out-of-control four wheeler? Electrical Rudolph on the rampage? Nothing unusual, just Wally doing last-minute Christmas shopping . . . FOR GOD! Chaos and comedy follow as he turns the town upside down looking for the perfect gift.
(ISBN 0-8499-3866-x)

#10—*My Life As a Toasted Time Traveler*

Wally travels back from the future to warn himself of an upcoming accident. But before he knows it, there are more Wallys running around than even Wally himself can handle. (ISBN 0-8499-3867-8)

#11—*My Life As Polluted Pond Scum*

This laugh-filled Wally disaster includes: a monster lurking in the depths of a mysterious lake . . . a glowing figure with powers to summon the creature to the shore . . . and one Wally McDoogle, who reluctantly stumbles upon the truth. Wally's entire town is in danger. He must race against the clock, his own fears, and learn to trust God before he has any chance of saving the day. (ISBN 0-8499-3875-9)

#12—*My Life As a Bigfoot Breath Mint*

Wally gets his big break to star with his uncle Max in the famous Fantasmo World stunt show. Unlike his father, whom Wally secretly suspects to be a major loser, Uncle Max is everything Wally longs to be . . . or so it appears. But Wally soon discovers the truth and learns who the real hero is in his life. (ISBN 0-8499-3876-7)

#13—*My Life As a Blundering Ballerina*

Wally agrees to switch places with Wall Street. Everyone is in on the act as the two try to survive seventy-two hours in each other's shoes and learn the importance of respecting other people. (ISBN 0-8499-4022-2)

#14—*My Life As a Screaming Skydiver*

Master of mayhem Wally turns a game of laser tag into international espionage. From the Swiss Alps to the African plains, Agent 00½th bumblingly employs such top-secret gizmos as rocket-powered toilet paper, exploding dental floss, and the ever-popular transformer tacos to stop the dreaded and super secret . . . Giggle Gun. (ISBN 0-8499-4023-0)

#15—*My Life As a Human Hairball*

When Wally and Wall Street visit a local laboratory, they are accidentally miniaturized and swallowed by some unknown stranger. It is a race against the clock as they fly through various parts of the body in a desperate search for a way out while learning how wonderfully we're made. (ISBN 0-8499-4024-9)

16—*My Life As a Walrus Whoopee Cushion*

Wally and his buddies, Opera and Wall Street, win the Gazillion Dollar Lotto! Everything is great, until they realize they lost the ticket at the zoo! Add some bungling bad guys, a zoo break-in, the release of all the animals, a SWAT team or two . . . and you have the usual McDoogle mayhem as Wally learns the dangers of greed.
(ISBN 0-8499-4025-7)

Look for this humorous fiction series
at your local Christian bookstore.